SANJAY'S STORY

Bloomsbury Education
An imprint of Bloomsbury Publishing Plc

50 Bedford Square
London
WC1B 3DP
UK

1385 Broadway
New York
NY 10018
USA

www.bloomsbury.com

BLOOMSBURY and the Diana logo are trademarks of Bloomsbury Publishing Plc

First published in Great Britain 2017
This paperback edition published in 2017

A catalogue record for this book is available from the British Library.

ISBN: PB: 978-1-4729-3483-3
ePub: 978-1-4729-3480-2
ePDF: 978-1-4729-3482-6

2 4 6 8 10 9 7 5 3 1

Typeset by Integra Software Services Pvt. Ltd.
Printed and bound in China by Leo Paper Products.

To find out more about our authors and books visit www.bloomsbury.com. Here you
will find extracts, author interviews, details of forthcoming events and the option to
sign up for our newsletters.

recommended by

www.catchup.org

Catch Up is a charity which aims to address the problem of underachievement that
has its roots in literacy and numeracy difficulties

JUDY WAITE

SANJAY'S STORY

Illustrated by Chris Askham

BLOOMSBURY EDUCATION
AN IMPRINT OF BLOOMSBURY

LONDON OXFORD NEW YORK NEW DELHI SYDNEY

THE STREET

Lena, Kai, Sanjay and Chelsea live on Swatton High Street.

They are fourteen years old, and they are best friends. They'll never let each other down...

CONTENTS

Smashed

Hi Sanjay – me and Chelsea are heading off to Kai's New Year party soon. It'll be buzzing. What time u finishing at work?

Lena xxx

Hi Lena – should make it 8-9pm. Dad said is OK for me to finish early even tho' we're busy :0)
Sanjay

Sanjay knew he should not be checking texts. He was supposed to be waiting on the customers. There was a group sitting at the table by the window. They were mostly girls, with one boy. The boy was scrolling through pictures of himself on his phone. They all looked a couple of years older than Sanjay.

One of the girls smiled at Sanjay. "Help me choose what to order," she said.

Sanjay gave a bow. "You're cute," she giggled.

Sanjay looked at her properly. She was more than cute. She was beautiful. She had long brown hair and slanted green eyes.

She waved the menu in his face. "What's Chicken Badam Pasanda?"

Sanjay wanted to say something funny to make her giggle again, but he could not think of anything. "Creamy chicken with ground almonds," he answered.

"Almonds? So it's nutty chicken?" she joked.

"That's it." Sanjay suddenly flapped his arms and made squawking sounds. "Nutty chicken."

The girl raised her eyebrows. "Amazing 'chicken-flap' dance moves," she said.

"You should see me do the wild-lemon-lamb," Sanjay grinned.

"Don't make me wait a second longer!" said the girl.

Sanjay took a few steps that were a cross between a hop and a moonwalk. His brother, Dipak, shook his head at Sanjay.

All of the girl's friends were clapping

"Do you work here every night?" the girl asked.

"Weekends and school holidays," Sanjay replied. He couldn't stop grinning. He knew he probably looked like a total idiot, but no one had ever called him cute before. It was a moment to be celebrated.

"That sucks," the girl said as she twizzled a strand of hair round her finger.

"I still get to go out," said Sanjay. "One of my best mates is having a party tonight. I'll be going soon." Sanjay had a sudden thought. Maybe she'd go to the party with him. Did he have the guts to ask her?

The boy scowled at Sanjay. "Are you hitting on Juliet?" he asked. "Do you think she'd be into scrawny schoolboys?" He laughed. Sanjay saw him flex his muscles beneath his shirt.

"Oh, back off, Mack," said Juliet. She rolled her eyes at the boy. "He can hit on me if he wants to. It's a free country."

Mack looked sulky. "You seem to get guys following you around everywhere you go."

This time it was Juliet who laughed. "Lucky me."

Juliet's friends laughed with her. "Lucky Juliet."

Sanjay guessed Mack was either already Juliet's boyfriend, or Mack hoped he would be by the end of the evening. He clearly didn't like her joking around with other guys.

Sanjay wasn't someone who looked for trouble.

"Are you ready to order, or shall I give you all a few more minutes?" Sanjay asked. He smiled, but this was his fake waiter's smile. He was careful not to look at Juliet again.

Suddenly there was a bang. Something hit the window. The glass seemed to shake, then crack.

Juliet screamed. Her friends screamed too. Mack leapt up and dived under the table.

Bricks and Bhajis

"Something's been thrown from outside," said Sanjay. He knew he had to sound calm. "Our window is made of special glass. Don't worry, it won't fall in on you."

The window was shattered but the glass was firm.

"Maybe it's an angry customer who got served a rotten onion bhaji," said Mack. He climbed back out from under the table.

Juliet started giggling, as if she hadn't been scared at all. "Maybe it was the onion bhaji that got thrown."

Mack smirked. "I vote we don't **curry** on eating here. The Crown pub up the street does two-for-one deals."

"OK. I'm up for that." Juliet stood up and put on her jacket. Her friends did the same.

Mack turned to Sanjay. "Sorry mate, but we're doing you a favour," he said. "You'll get more time to finish your homework."

Sanjay smiled his waiter's smile. He still couldn't look at Juliet. He wished he could tell Mack what he really thought of him. Mack was a wimp, hiding under the table.

"Enjoy your meal at The Crown," Sanjay said politely. Chelsea, one of Sanjay's best mates, lived at The Crown. Her mum had just done it up, and the whole two-for-one thing was very popular. He looked around his dad's restaurant. It seemed old-fashioned. Even the name The Curry House seemed boring.

There were some paintings he had done at primary school on the wall. He had painted three magic snakes. Mum had them framed. He had been so proud. He wanted the rest of his family to comment, but only his oldest brother, Hari, ever said anything. He called Sanjay 'snake slime' for a few weeks, until he got bored and thought up some new insults.

Sanjay's dad came over and spoke to Juliet and her friends. "Please, there is no need for anyone to go. There is no danger," he said.

But everyone pushed past him.

"Have you called the police?" Hari said to Dipak.

"Yes, but they couldn't say when they will get here," Dipak replied. "New Year's Eve is a busy night for them."

Sanjay knew that the police would not make any difference anyway. Whoever had smashed their window would not be hanging around.

Dad turned to Hari. "Go outside and check the damage," he said. "You too, Sanjay."

Sanjay and Hari went out onto the street. "No onion bhajis," muttered Sanjay.

"What are you talking about now?" Hari said. He pointed at a brick in the gutter. "That's what got thrown."

Juliet walked past Sanjay. She didn't even look at him as she left with her friends. Mack had his arm round Juliet. Sanjay felt a twist in his chest. This was crazy. He didn't even know her. Why did he feel so gutted?

"You might as well go back in," said Hari. "You're a waste of space here."

Sanjay went back into The Curry House.

Customers were paying bills and getting ready to leave. Dad kept offering them free drinks, but no one was interested. Sanjay felt sad. His parents worked hard. They didn't deserve to have vandals messing everything up.

Dad saw him and hurried over. "Is it very bad?"

"Yes, it is," Sanjay said. But he didn't mean the window damage. He meant the way life sometimes felt like a rotten onion bhaji.

Snake Charmer

Sanjay worked hard clearing plates. He couldn't stop thinking about Juliet.

"Hey, stop daydreaming," said Dipak. "There's a dirty table over there. You need to sort it out." Dipak clicked his fingers in Sanjay's face.

Sanjay felt like biting them.

He went over to the dirty table. Was this really his life? His future? He wanted to be an artist. It was his best subject at school but Dad said Sanjay needed a business brain. Dad thought art was a waste of time.

Suddenly Sanjay remembered Lena's text about the party. He needed to get changed.

Dipak was serving a young couple.

"Dad promised I could go out," Sanjay whispered to him.

Dipak shrugged. "It's not as if you care about this place," he said. "If you hadn't been messing around, you might have seen who smashed our window."

Sanjay turned away. Stuff Dipak and Hari. They were Dad's golden boys. None of his family understood him.

Running up the stairs, Sanjay undid his tie. His thirteen-year-old sister, Papri, appeared. "You finished work?" she asked.

"You bet. Now I'm off to a party!" Sanjay said.

He bounded into his bedroom, pulling off the waiter's uniform. Now he was a snake-boy, shedding a skin. Pulling on his jeans and tee shirt, he crept down to the hall and past the kitchen.

The pans on the cookers were steaming, but there was no sign of Dad or his brothers.

Mum was chopping vegetables, but she had her back to Sanjay.

Sanjay grabbed his jacket and opened the back door. The night was cold. The sky was bright with stars.

"Sanjay, we know there are bad gangs out tonight," Mum said, appearing behind him. "Maybe you should stay home?"

Sanjay paused. How was it Mum seemed to know everything that was going on?

"I'm only going to Kai's party," said Sanjay. He let the door slam with a bang.

He liked the angry sound it made.

Maybe that was the same thrill vandals got from smashing windows?

Street Party

Kai's place wasn't far away. The street was busy, but Sanjay could hear music blaring out.

Chelsea appeared in the hall as Sanjay stepped inside the house. She smiled. "Hi Sanjay. You made it." Kai wandered out from the kitchen.

He was eating a chicken drumstick. He clapped Sanjay on the shoulder. "Good to see you. This party needs a bit of your crazy style."

Chelsea hugged Sanjay. "We've missed you." She dragged him towards the front room. "Lena is here with a bunch of people from school."

Lena spotted Sanjay as he hesitated in the doorway. "Sanjay!" she smiled. "You got away from work at last. I did a double shift at the café today too. Sucks, doesn't it? Come and show these guys your moonwalk. Everybody make space for Sanjay!"

But as the music thumped and thudded, Sanjay realised he didn't want to moonwalk. He didn't want to do the chicken–flap or the wild–lemon–lamb. Being the crazy one was just another way of looking like an idiot.

"Sorry," said Sanjay. "I have just realised there's something I need to do. I need to go."

"You've only just arrived," Lena said. She turned to Kai. "Make him stay," she begged.

"You can't abandon us," laughed Kai, waving the chicken drumstick dramatically. "We need your mad dance moves."

Sanjay shook his head. "I'll catch you later," he said.

Seconds later he was running down the street. His trainers bashed out their own musical beat. Thump thud thump thud thump thud.

He slowed as he neared the jewellery shop.

A shop stashed with treasures.

Sanjay could hide in the jewellery shop doorway until midnight, then go home and pretend he'd had an awesome night out.

No one would know the truth.

He moved into the shadowy doorway and sat on the cold step. His phone kept buzzing with texts from Lena and Chelsea, so he turned it off.

He shuffled his legs to one side and tried to get comfortable – then he kicked something soft. Sanjay felt panic twist in his gut.

Someone was there. He knew tramps often slept in shop doorways. "Um... sorry," Sanjay muttered. He struggled to get up but his foot seemed to be looped in something. His heart pounded in panic. "Let me go, please. I don't want any trouble."

There was silence. Sanjay put his hand out. He touched a soft, rough shape. Not a human. It was a backpack.

Maybe someone had dumped it here? Maybe the bag was full of stolen jewellery from the shop. This would mean a massive reward.

Sanjay picked up the backpack and ran along the street. Music was still blaring from Kai's place. He dodged past a skip filled with rubbish, then headed for the alley that led to the park. Bad things sometimes happened in alleys. They were dark and shadowy. If there were gangs about, Sanjay wouldn't stand a chance.

But he wanted to be somewhere quiet. He needed to know what was stashed in that backpack.

Paint Job

Sanjay stopped half way along the alley. A street lamp cast a yellow light across the old brick wall.

He knelt beside the backpack and undid the straps. Reaching inside, his hand touched something cold. A cylinder.

His heart sank as he pulled out the first can.

It was spray paint. Stupid useless spray paint.

Sanjay held the can high. He undid the cap and pressed the nozzle. There was a hiss and the smell of paint. The paint hit the alley wall.

Sanjay pressed the nozzle again.

He waved his hand around, spraying a giant yellow 'S' onto the bricks. He pulled out more cans. New colours. The 'S' became a snake. A magical snake, patterned with jewels.

Art at school had never made Sanjay feel like this. It was as if he owned the wall.

Maybe he owned the whole world. He was a spray-can superhero, with colours shooting out of his fingertips.

He worked faster. He sprayed green eyes. He sprayed a screaming mouth.

He gave the snake fangs. It looked angry. Ready to strike.

"Where are you, Juliet? Come and watch this," Sanjay muttered as he sprayed. "You can't **curry** on making fun of me now. Stuff you. Stuff that wimpy boyfriend too. Look at me. LOOK at me."

He stepped back and stared at his work. His masterpiece. "Look at me," he muttered again.

Then he heard a soft voice. "I am looking at you," it said.

Scar Face

Sanjay dropped the spray can.

He pictured the police turning up at The Curry House and arresting him. Dad would shout. Mum would cry. His brothers would be disgusted. Sanjay turned to see who had crept up on him.

It was a tramp. His clothes looked as though he'd dug them out of that skip. His face was dirty and his long hair was matted.

"You've been working hard." The tramp nodded at the wall.

It was covered in twirling snakes, green eyes and screaming mouths. "I can clean it off," Sanjay mumbled.

"Not easily." The tramp shook his head. "At least you haven't signed it. The police won't have any clues."

He took a step nearer to Sanjay. He had a silver scar that ran from his eye to his chin.

"Keep away from me," Sanjay said. He snatched the backpack up, holding it in front of him like a shield. "I've got stuff in here that could hurt you."

The tramp held out his hand. "I only want..." he began.

"You're scum," yelled Sanjay. He wasn't going wait to find out what the tramp wanted. He turned and ran, racing out of the alley.

There were fireworks in the distance. They looked like jewels exploding in the sky.

Further along the street, the music at Kai's house was still booming.

Sanjay just wanted to be home. He raced to the safety of The Curry House.

Monsters Under the Bed

Sanjay couldn't sleep. The backpack was like a monster in the room. He had pushed it under his bed, but it was not hidden very well. Mum or Dad would find it if they came to change his bedding. He would have to dump it in the skip tomorrow.

He looked out of the window. The midnight fireworks were all finished and the street was quiet. The sky was still clear, and it looked icy outside.

Sanjay wondered where the tramp was sleeping. Was he warm enough? Maybe all he had been doing was begging for a few coins. Sanjay had called him 'scum'. He felt ashamed of himself.

Sanjay's dad had been homeless when he was a teenager. Dad said it was a terrible time but it taught him never to judge anyone else. Life could be hard sometimes.

"I'm sorry, Mr Tramp," Sanjay whispered into the darkness. "I'll get food for you. I can deliver you a hot takeaway. I'll do my best to find you again."

Sanjay fell asleep with that thought.

Cheated

It was the next day: New Year's Day. Sanjay was walking along the street. Lena was outside Street-Level, a music place that was closed down for repairs. She was playing with her puppy, Robbie. Kai stood beside her, checking his phone.

"Hey, Sanjay." Lena waved at him. "I've sent you about a zillion texts," she said.

Kai looked up. "Me too. You haven't answered any of our messages," he said.

Sanjay gave them both a fake grin. He had just dumped the backpack in the skip. "I – er – my battery's flat," he said.

"Muppet. You should be more organised," said Lena. "We're going back to mine. We were up all night and we need caffeine, badly. You up for that?"

"Um – not sure," Sanjay answered. He had begged a takeaway from Mum.

He planned to check the park. Tramps sometimes hung out there.

"**Please**. Kai's off to kickboxing training soon, and Chelsea's brother Tommy is home from the army so Chelsea's doing family stuff," said Lena. "I'm in danger of spending New Year's Day watching telly with Mum and Dad." She ran her finger down her cheek, pretending there was a tear running down it.

The action reminded Sanjay of the tramp. That scar. He needed to get the takeaway to him while it was hot. "I've got things to do," he said.

Just then, a flashy silver car drew up.

"Cool car," whistled Kai. "A Porsche."

"Maybe it's someone famous," Lena breathed. "We could get a selfie."

"I really need to go," said Sanjay, but then his words stuck in his throat.

The driver got out.

He was in a smart suit. His hair was clean and pulled back in a ponytail.

But it was the scar that did it.

It ran down his face like a silver tear. It was the tramp!

Sanjay scowled. "Cheat," he muttered. The tramp was not really a tramp at all.

He must be making a fortune from begging. Sanjay wished he could shout out the truth, but the tramp might shout back. He might tell everyone what he had seen Sanjay doing.

Sanjay chucked the takeaway into the skip. The whole world stank of scar-faced liars. Stuff feeling sorry for tramps! He had just been an idiot again.

He turned back to Lena. "Come on then, let's go and have a coffee at your house."

He was still angry, and the anger was like a snake uncoiling. He needed time to think about what he was going to do.

Looking for Trouble

Sanjay looked out through Lena's back room window. It was a misty evening. "I need to leave," he said to Lena. "Mum said I had to be home early tonight."

This wasn't true. Mum was always saying Dad made him work too much.

She liked knowing he was with his mates.

Lena's mum and dad had the telly on in the kitchen. Sanjay called goodbye to them. They didn't answer. The telly was on too loud.

"See you tomorrow?" asked Lena.

"OK." Sanjay nodded. He could not think about tomorrow. He was not heading home at all. He had a plan, and he was buzzing with it, but it wasn't something he could tell Lena about.

Sanjay hugged Lena goodbye, then stepped into the mist.

"Bye bye, gorgeous boy," called Lena.

Sanjay turned and waved.

He did the 'chicken–flap' and the 'wild–lemon–lamb' for her. He moonwalked backwards along the street, still waving.

"Sanjay, you're mad, but brilliant," Lena said in a sing–song voice.

Next door, Kai's bedroom light was not on. This meant there was a good chance he was out somewhere. Great. Sanjay didn't want to hang out with Kai tonight.

He kept moonwalking backwards... right into a couple who were snogging outside the kebab shop.

"Hey! Watch it!" said the boy.

"Look where you're going," said the girl.

The boy swung round to face up to Sanjay, but it wasn't him Sanjay was looking at. It was Juliet.

Sanjay felt his heart thump. How was it she made him feel this way?

"You?" she said, stepping forward to get a better look. "That cute schoolboy waiter from The Curry House?"

Sanjay glanced from her face, to the boy's, and blurted out, "You've moved on from that wimpy boy then?"

"What are you talking about?" Juliet frowned.

"You were with a different boy last night," said Sanjay. "The – er – the one who hid under the table. I think that was pretty wimpy."

He knew he was saying the wrong thing, but she'd made him feel flustered. He was back to being that idiot waiter again.

"Oh, you mean Mack?" Juliet said, and turned to the boy she'd just been wrapped round. "Someone chucked a brick at The Curry House window and Mack got freaked out by it. It was really funny."

"You didn't say Mack was going to be at The Curry House," said the boy. He sounded angry. "You said it was a girls' night."

"Mack showed up. So what? Are you saying I can't talk to other guys?" said Juliet.

"Not when you've said it was a girls' night. And not when that guy is Mack Katan," said the boy.

"You don't own me," Juliet said. She put her hands on her hips and glared at the boy.

"I can't see why you're interested in Muscles–Mack," said the boy. "He's boring."

Juliet rolled her eyes. "You're just jealous," she said. "Maybe he thinks you're boring, too."

Sanjay looked at them both. Things clearly weren't going well, but Juliet seemed more than up to dealing with this new bully. She didn't need him hanging about.

"Anyway," he said, holding one hand up. "Good to have – er – bumped into you. See you around."

Juliet didn't answer. She was still arguing with the boy.

Sanjay was glad he hadn't had the guts to ask Juliet to come to Kai's party. She would probably have ended up with loads of guys after her. He reached the skip. It was dark now, and hard to see what was inside. He ran his hand over the bags and boxes. Sanjay was fed up of being good, when scumbag types got away with being bad.

He was going to treat himself to one night of perfect badness.

His fingers brushed the buckles of the backpack. This was his moment. He would transform into a snake-boy.

"Come on, my friendssss," Snake-boy hissed as he pulled the backpack from the skip. "We're off to decorate the sssports hut in the park. I'm looking for trouble."

Gang Land

Sanjay turned off the main street and headed to the park. The mist seemed even thicker there. The trees were ghostly. The swings and slide looked fuzzy. He walked towards the sports hut.

He took a spray-can from the backpack, but he didn't feel so brave now. Anyone could creep up on him. Anyone – or anything.

"Just do it," he whispered to himself. "Stop being a goof." His voice sounded strange in the quiet.

He pressed his finger on the nozzle.

He couldn't see clearly but he could sense the whoosh of paint. He moved his hand in an 'S' shape. He would cover the hut with snakes. 'Slimy Snake-boy' would make his mark.

Only then, he heard thumps and yells. Something was being dragged towards the sports hut.

Another thump. A groan. "Please, don't do this," said a man's voice. He sounded desperate.

"Vermin like you should be stamped out," a different voice said.

"Stamped on," added another.

It sounded as though the man was being pushed about. Sanjay crouched low, hoping he wouldn't be noticed.

"You're scum," the first voice hissed.

"Filthy," yelled another.

How big was this gang? Sanjay saw it was a group of guys. They looked as if they were in their late teens or early twenties. They seemed to be dragging the man with them.

Suddenly Sanjay knew he couldn't just leave while some stranger got beaten up. His heart thundered. If they turned on him, he'd be beaten too.

"Stop!" he yelled. His voice seemed to boom in the mist. "If you don't stop, I'll blind you." He sprayed the can randomly. The paint hissed. The smell stung the misty air.

Sanjay saw someone move towards him. The guy called out, "It's just spray paint." But he sounded uncertain. Sanjay took a second can from the backpack.

Sanjay sprayed again.

"This stuff is acid. It won't just blind you, it'll melt your eyes," he said.

"It smells strong," a new voice muttered.

Sanjay pressed the nozzles. They hissed like snakes. "I'm warning you," said Sanjay. "This can burn your guts up."

"Sounds to me like you're all alone here," said one of the gang. "You've made a BIG mistake." Foggy figures were walking towards him. They moved slowly, like a gang of ghosts.

Sanjay swallowed. "It'll blister your lungs," he said.

He pressed harder on the nozzles... but suddenly both cans stopped sizzling. They were empty.

Idiot! Sanjay was shaking as he bent to grab the next can.

But he was too late.

"Run out of ammunition?" Four of the gang were standing round him. The others stayed in the background still holding onto whoever it was they had dragged into the park. The gang started pushing Sanjay, shoving him from one to the other of them. He stumbled against the side of the sports hut.

"Oh look, he's on his knees," laughed one.

"Beg for mercy, loser," said another.

They pushed him face down onto the grass.

Sanjay curled into a ball, waiting for the first kick.

Then, there was another shout. A voice he knew. "Get off him!" It was Kai.

Sanjay rolled over, just in time to see Kai aim one of his super kicks close to the nearest gang-member's backside. "Hey, what the..."

Kai kicked again. He didn't make contact, but Sanjay knew that was on purpose. He could have knocked the thug over if he'd wanted to.

"What is this? Who's this maniac?" The other three backed away.

Sanjay stood up as another familiar voice rang through the hazy night.

This time it was Chelsea. "My friend's a black belt," she said. "He's the kickboxing champion from Spitting Tiger gym. The whole team are on their way over here to practise on all of you." Chelsea walked over to them. She stood with her arms folded. From the way her chin tilted, Sanjay could tell she was glaring.

The gang hesitated. "You think we're bothered?" said the nearest one. He picked up a drink can from the ground and went to throw it at Chelsea.

Kai leapt at him, kicking the can away. It spun up onto the sports hut roof.

Another gang member laughed. "Good shot."

The guy who had held the can sounded furious. "You think that's funny, Joel? He could have smashed my fingers," he said. He turned and shoved Joel. Joel pushed back, then broke free and began to run. The whole gang followed, whooping and shouting.

Their footsteps made a thump thump thudding as they ran off.

"Cowards. They were looking for an excuse to escape," said Sanjay.

"They were scared the Spitting Tiger team were on their way," Chelsea agreed. "They weren't really. I made it up."

"I liked it that you gave me champion status," Kai said to her. "You made that up, too."

"Well, you will be one day, I'm sure." Chelsea turned to Sanjay, "Are you OK?" she asked. She shone the torch from her mobile into his face.

"Just about. How did you find me?" said Sanjay.

"Chelsea's brother, Tommy, was in Dad's taxi, on his way back to army camp," said Kai.

"Tommy saw you rummaging through a skip as they drove by," Chelsea went on. "He texted to ask if you were always a bit weird. I said that you were wonderfully crazy. Then we started thinking it was more crazy than normal, so we came looking. Good job we did."

There were footsteps, and someone new stepped forward. "Good job indeed. I reckon forensics would have been wiping our body parts off the grass in the morning," he said.

Chelsea shone her phone towards the speaker.

It was the tramp. His clothes were torn.

His matted hair was full of leaves. "Thank you. All three of you," he said. He turned to Sanjay. "You faced that gang to stick up for me. That was true bravery. I owe you."

Sanjay could see the tramp was grateful, but he felt angry. "The first thing you owe me is an explanation," he said.

Chelsea frowned at Sanjay, then turned to the tramp. "You look like you've been in a fight too."

"I was about to be beaten up but your friend threatened them with spray paints. He was really brave."

"It was a gut reaction," Sanjay snapped. "I wouldn't have stepped in if I'd known it was you."

"That's harsh, Sanjay. This guy looks down on his luck to me. What's your problem?" asked Kai.

"He's not who you think he is," replied Sanjay. He scowled at the tramp and said, "I saw you earlier. In your silver car."

"Ah, I see." The tramp brushed dead leaves from his jacket. "I can explain everything. Can we all go somewhere and talk this through?"

Home Truths

The four of them sat in Kai's kitchen.

"So," Sanjay said, sipping a coffee. "Who, what, and why?" He couldn't look at the tramp. He still didn't trust him.

"My name's Adam Allsop," said the tramp.

"OK." Sanjay shrugged.

"I'm not really homeless," said Adam. He stirred his own coffee. "I'm a journalist," he went on. "I wanted to write an article about being homeless at New Year. I thought the best way was to try it for myself. Rough myself up a bit. Stay out all night..."

Sanjay frowned. "Why should I believe that? I bet you beg for money. I bet that's how you bought that silver car."

"That was you in the Porsche we saw yesterday?" Kai whistled. "Nice work."

Sanjay rolled his eyes. "Not nice work. He tricks people into believing he's a poor helpless tramp," he said.

Adam shook his head. "I didn't trick anyone," he said. "I just slept rough. I... er... my family is well off. My dad got me that Porsche. I don't like it much, to be honest. I don't want to be given things. Writing good articles about real people matters more."

Kai raised his eyebrows. "You don't like the Porsche? You're nearly as crazy as Sanjay," he said.

Sanjay stared at Adam. He understood about dads who wanted different things for their sons. Things the sons might not want. He swigged the last of his coffee and sat back in his chair.

"So, how did you get the scar?" Sanjay asked Adam. He suddenly hoped it was something heroic. He hoped Adam had been rescuing polar bears from melting ice caps or something.

"Fell off a motorbike," grinned Adam. "A big beast of a bike. A BMW. Another of my dad's unwanted gifts."

"No way!" Kai laughed. He was looking at Adam as though he had just been beamed down from Mars. "You get any more of those unwanted gifts, just give me a call," he said.

Adam turned to Sanjay.

"That graffiti the other night was impressive. I've been working on another article about some ex-prisoners. They've put a team together called Smart Arts and they work as legit graffiti artists, painting subways and bridges and things. I've just got them some work."

Sanjay could feel Kai and Chelsea staring at him. They didn't know anything about Snake-boy. "What sort of work?" Sanjay asked.

"My brother Matthew bought Street-Level last year," explained Adam. "You know, the music place? Matthew has booked Smart Arts to redecorate the place."

Adam finished his coffee and looked at Sanjay. "I could get you into that Smart Arts team," he said.

Shine On

"You need to control the line of spray coming out of the can," Tamsin said as she sprayed white paint onto the warehouse wall. "Watch... this way, I get a thick line, but I can get really fine lines too."

Sanjay watched as Tamsin added more detail, and more colours.

"Cool," Sanjay said, nodding as the picture became clear. "A massive unicorn. You made it look so easy."

"Nice work, Tamsin," said Jonjo, coming over to join them. Jonjo was in charge of the Street Smart team. "Your turn, Sanjay. Spray that wall there. It doesn't matter if you make a mistake."

Five minutes later Sanjay was spraying wiggly lines of yellow. "I can't believe I'm allowed to do this," he grinned.

"It's my dream job," said Jonjo.

"Ours too." Two more members of the team, Colin and Gemma, walked over to watch.

"Just go for it," said Gemma. "You'll be OK."

Sanjay picked up another can. He sprayed a black background around the wiggles of yellow.

"That's it, just sort of feel your way through it," said Jonjo. "Let it flow."

Sanjay sprayed stronger wiggles of yellow so they were over the top of the black.

"Pretty good," said Jonjo.

"Nice work," said Tamsin.

But Sanjay was barely listening.

He filled the black background with stars. The stars were exploding, as if the gods had thrown bricks and cracked open the night sky.

He began to move as he worked. He was just walking at first, but soon he was doing a sort of cross between a hop and a moonwalk.

The others clapped. "This kid has amazing energy," laughed Colin.

Across the wall, Sanjay's stars were raining diamonds onto the yellow squiggles.

"You have painted three snakes twisted together," said Tasmin. "Is that your tag, Sanjay?" she said.

Sanjay stopped spraying.

"Yeah," he said. "It is my tag. It stands for Snake-Shine Sanjay."

Smart Art

Matthew Allsop stepped onto the stage inside Street-Level. "Thank you all for coming," he said. "This place looks incredible, and that is down to a lot of hard work from talented people."

Sanjay stood at the back of the stage with the rest of the team.

Matthew Allsop was still talking. "The Smart Arts team have given this place the graffiti makeover of my dreams. Guys – step forward."

Sanjay saw Mum and Papri waving.

His brothers grinned.

Dad, in his best suit, was puffed up with pride.

"Wooo wooo!" Kai beat his fist in the air.

"We love you Sanjay!" shouted Chelsea.

Lena looked as if she might run up on the stage and hug him. "You smashed it, hun," she yelled.

It was as he was leaving the back of the stage that a girl stepped forward.

"Hi, cute boy," said the girl.

"Juliet?" Sanjay frowned.

Juliet giggled. "I wanted to say how awesome the graffiti is. I can't even draw a stick man. I think you're amazing."

She moved closer to Sanjay. "It would be good to hang out with you."

Sanjay felt that familiar twist in his heart.

Juliet was so beautiful. But then he remembered how she had gone off with that wimp, Mack. She had ignored Sanjay when she left The Curry House that night. She hadn't wanted to know him then.

"Sorry," he said. "My friends are waiting for me."

He did a few steps that were a cross between a hop and a moonwalk, then turned and walked away.

Bonus Bits!

What is graffiti?

Graffiti is writing or drawings scribbled, scratched or sprayed on a wall or other surfaces in a public place. This is against the law.

Some of the art that is created has gained recognition from the art world and is (in the right place and if agreed by the owner of the property) a legitimate form of art.

WHO'S WHO?

Match the sentence with the character that said it. Look back at the story if you need to. The answers are at the end of the section.

A "You should see me do the wild–lemon–lamb."

B "Are you hitting on Juliet?"

C "Don't make me wait a second longer."

D "There is no danger."

E "That's what got thrown."

F "It's not as if you care about this place."

G "You finished work?"

H "Maybe you should stay home."

1 Papri (Sanjay's sister)

2 Juliet

3 Sanjay

4 Hari (Sanjay's brother)

5 Sanjay's mum

6 Mack

7 Dipak (Sanjay's brother)

8 Sanjay's dad

INTERESTING WORDS

Here are a few words you might not know from this story.

coward someone who does not have the courage to do or endure something dangerous or unpleasant.

vandals people who deliberately destroy or damage something that belongs to someone else.

gangs groups of people who join together to do criminal acts.

moonwalk a dance with a gliding motion where the dancer looks as if he or she is moving forwards when he or she is actually moving backwards.

bully   someone who is unkind to someone else, using their strength or influence to intimidate them.

vermin   animals which are harmful to crops or other animals, or which carry diseases, e.g. rats.

forensics   science tests or techniques used to study crimes to identify the person who did it or the way it was done.

WHAT NEXT?

If you enjoyed reading this story and haven't already read *Chelsea's Story*, grab yourself a copy and curl up somewhere to read it!

ANSWERS to WHO'S WHO?

A3, B6, C2, D8, E4, F7, G1, H5